FAIRY TALES AND OTHER STORIES
BY A CENTENARIAN

Margaret E. F. Llewellyn Smith

Fairy Tales and Other Stories by a Centenarian

By Margaret Emily Frances Llewellyn Smith,
resident of the Old Vicarage, Moulsford
composed in her 100th, 101st and 102nd years

Illustrated by Colette Llewellyn Smith

TASTON BOOKS

First published in 2007 by
Taston Books
Brook Cottage, Taston OX7 3JL

ISBN 978-0-9554601-0-4

Designed and typeset by Jon Carpenter 01608 811969
Manufactured in the UK by LPPS Ltd, Wellingborough NN8 3PJ

Contents

The Author, at the Old Vicarage, Moulsford

The Babies' Parliament

The gardens were illuminated by brilliant moonlight. It glowed on the fronts of the old houses round the Square. Gradually, the sound of the traffic in the street died away. Before long, a new sound broke the silence. It was the pattering of little feet, and out came the babies clutching their night gowns or baby-grows up to their knees. They gathered on the dry grass and sat in a ring round their leader Roderick. He rose, clapped his hands together for silence, and addressed the Assembly. He spoke quietly, so as not to draw the attention of any grown-ups in the surrounding houses.

'This is the last time I shall be president of this Assembly of Babies. As most of you know, I shall be two years old tomorrow and will be no more eligible to join you. I shall be very sorry to leave you, but I am looking forward to growing up. Now – I have the pleasant duty of introducing a new member, Fiona.' A very small baby was given a push by her neighbours, rose and murmured a shy 'Thank You.'

Roderick continued: 'Shall we talk baby talk or grown-up talk?' 'I don't know any grown-up talk' said Fiona. 'Doesn't your mother speak to you when she's feeding you?' asked Roderick. 'No, she never talks to me. She just sticks a bottle in my mouth. Then it falls out, and she rushes in again and says 'Tiresome child!' and sticks it in again. And it's quite cold, but it's all I get. My Granny talks to me, but she always says the same things like "Sweetie Baby, Darling Child, her old Granny loves her if nobody else does!"'

The talk then became general. It was mostly discussion of parents or nannies. After some time had passed, Roderick spoke again: 'As most of you know, this enchanted hour will end when the clock next strikes.

You must be back in your cots before then. We must leave not a trace of our presence here.' Silently, the Assembly broke up and the babies toddled back to their respective houses.

On the following afternoon, the square garden was occupied by mothers, nurses and some children who ran about and did not appear to feel the heat though their elders sought the shade. There were also a few dogs confined to an area reserved for them. They were usually

peaceful, but sometimes fights broke out and then the owners – treading warily – had to venture in to separate them.

Meanwhile Roderick, in one of the great old houses round the Square, was being prepared for his birthday party. He was given a clean shirt, his hair was brushed, and he was admonished by his Mother to say 'Ta!' for his presents. 'Ta' was one of the few words he could speak in baby talk, although he still understood grown-up speech, and because he was listening hard he forgot the 'Ta' on the first occasion.

His first presents were from his brothers and sister. They were modest, because they were bought with the children's own small pocket money – two pencils with Roderick's name on them and a jolly pop-up card. Roderick liked things with his name on them. They gave him a sense of pride of ownership. Roderick appreciated even the present from his elderly Godfather, which he would otherwise have regarded as boring. It was a mug with his name on it and exactly the same as last year's present. But it was acceptable, because the last one had been broken a few days before.

After the party, Roderick was tucked up in the small bed to which he had been promoted from his cot some weeks earlier. His Mother told him to turn over and to go to sleep 'Because you must be tired, Darling.' Roderick obeyed the first part of this instruction, but he was too excited for the second. He could not go to sleep. So he lay and thought over the lovely presents he had received – a farm with animals (rather beyond his scope at the moment), lots of bricks which he loved building towers with and knocking them down; two beautiful pull-along toys, a train and a bus which could be attached to each other at will.

The clock struck for the first time. Roderick was still awake. The second stroke brought to his mind the babies gathering at that magic hour. They would be assembling just at that moment, under the guidance of his friend and successor Dominic. But Roderick himself was now a big boy, and never again would he be able to join The Babies' Parliament.

A Christmas Fairy Tale

The Baron had not always been bad, he had been a revered landlord and a respected and well-liked neighbour. But since the death of his sweet and gentle wife he had got worse. He oppressed his tenants and insulted his neighbours and gathered about him bold young men with whom he held riotous parties. However, he had one soft spot – his little daughter. He marked off an apartment in the castle where his men friends might never enter and persuaded a widowed aunt to live with her there and bring her up. He visited her every day early, before a drop of drink had passed his lips. He loved her dearly and she loved and respected him.

The aunt, a learned woman, taught the little Lady Sylvia her early lessons, and later professors were introduced from the nearest university. The good aunt represented to the Baron that Sylvia ought to have some young society so the great ballroom was cleaned and redecorated and young aristocrats were invited – at first to children's parties, then to great balls where the young men fancied themselves in love with Lady Sylvia as she grew into lovely young womanhood. She would have none of them until the Prince of a neighbouring state came and drew her affections. He asked her hand in marriage but received from the Father the same answer that others had heard – 'Ask me later, my boy, she is too young to think of it now'.

Lady Sylvia grew up to be a girl not only of ravishing beauty, but of good learning, good sense and – best of all – a good heart.

One day, when the Baron had made a successful raid on a noted cattle breeder in the neighbourhood and brought home a number of valuable cows, he decided to have a big hunt and a great feast afterwards. He went at break of day to say goodbye to his daughter and tell her he would be back quite early for the feast.

The hunting party rode away and Sylvia settled down to her usual employment. As day drew on she began to fret, and wonder if some accident had befallen them. At last, hearing the sound of the returning party, she jumped away from the restraining hand of her aunt in excitement and rushed out to the terrace. She cried 'Is anything wrong? You are so late!'

Just as she uttered the words – but we must go back to the events of the Baron's day!

The hunting party had not had the successful day they hoped for and it was late in the afternoon before they saw the familiar track of a single fawn. She bounded away and the wearied hounds could barely keep her in sight. At last she grew wearied too, and in a distant and

unknown glade they made a kill. As they were loading the body onto the pack pony an old woman came out of a small cottage shouting furious abuse. The Baron laughed at her weird and surly appearance but the men, sensing that she was a witch, muttered nervously and some even crossed themselves. 'Brutes! Villains!' screamed the old dame! 'Brutes to kill my pet creature. I lay my curse on you! The first creature you meet on your return home shall turn into a deer and vanish from you. Brutes and villains!!'

Weary and dispirited, the party made its way home, where Sylvia ran out to meet them. Just as she called her greeting the beautiful girl vanished and a white hind was seen in her place. All the people stood rigid with horror, giving the creature time to dart away before anyone started in pursuit. It was too late. There was by then no sight of her.

There was great lamentation in the castle and in the countryside, near and far, for everyone loved the gentle and beautiful girl. Search parties were sent out, the Baron himself, discarding his wild ways and companions, leading one of them. All through that spring and summer they hunted, but as the first frosts of autumn came on many began to lose heart and hope. When the trees and bushes began to be rimy with hoarfrost the only searcher left was the Prince, who had vowed in his heart that never, as long as his life lasted, would he give up the search for this lost fawn.

One cold night as his tired horse stumbled along an obscure forest track he remembered that it was Christmas Eve. He remembered also an old legend he had heard that on that Holy Night the cattle in the stable had for one midnight hour lost their wild nature and worshipped with humans at the crib. And he heard strange rustlings in the undergrowth and thought he caught a glimpse of a wolf going peaceably beside a lamb. He wondered if they too were moved by some unusual inspiration. His own horse, too, refused to diverge from the direction the others were taking.

Suddenly a beam of light, brighter and more beautiful than any light he had ever seen, struck out from before them and as they all followed it they came to a tiny Chapel. At the open door, whence the light came, stood an old priest watching over a rough wooden cradle. At the door a crowd of animals were gathering and pressing up to the doorway where all knelt. The Prince and his horse knelt also and all listened attentively while the priest spoke holy words of Christmas. As he spoke the Prince perceived in the forefront of the throng a white hind. When the priest ceased speaking the Prince crept quietly forward, seized her round the neck and imprinted a fervent kiss upon her snowy forehead. Instantly, the miracle took place and Sylvia stood before him, more lovely he thought than he had ever seen her. He pressed her to him while the priest exorcised the evil magic and blessed them both, and they went out into the frosty air, after a prayer of thanks. There the horse – revived and lively – was ready to receive the double burden as the Prince lifted the slender girl onto the saddle bow before him.

The way home seemed quite short. When the castle was reached the rejoicing was such as none could remember. The Baron agreed to an immediate marriage and a magnificent wedding feast was quickly arranged.

The Prince and the Lady Sylvia settled in the Castle with the Baron and, as is usual in fairy stories, they all lived happily ever after.

College Magic

Late evening sunrays slanted over the college court turning the old grey buildings to a livelier glow, brightening the evening trees to a richer green. The sounds carried on the evening breeze seemed softer than the court's usual noises. Voices of young men and women from the far corner sounded musical and pleasing and even when a head came out of an upper window and someone shouted 'Shut up, can't you, I'm trying to work' it hardly seemed to ripple the sense of peace in that magical evening. A rush of glorious music from the chapel, where a music scholar was practising the organ, lifted the whole evening to a higher plane.

But the man walking along the path towards the dining hall appeared oblivious to the peace and beauty that surrounded him. His face was gloomy, eyes fixed on the ground, mouth set, and he offered no greeting to such people as he passed. For twenty-five years, since his young wife died, this man had withdrawn from any contact with the outside world that was not necessitated by his work. His work as a Professor of Classical Literature he performed conscientiously. His lectures were carefully prepared and clearly and audibly delivered. His tutorials were helpful and informative. But there was no greeting for his students, no farewell, no friendly interest in their interests and pursuits.

People called him The Recluse.

He went into Hall, and after a cursory bow to the President, who was already seated, he took a place as far down the table as he could. Lively conversation ensued between colleagues, an amicable group of men and women who had long since given up any attempt to draw him in. When the meal was over he made as swift a departure after the long Latin Grace as courtesy permitted and started on the walk back to his rooms.

Eyes on the ground as usual, he did not see what it was that hit his shins and threw him off balance. He fell lightly onto the grass, was unhurt, and rose quickly, hardly needing the proffered hand of a passing undergraduate and in time to see a handsome child pursuing a well-kicked football which had travelled away for some yards.

The child's mother was hurrying up to offer apologies and it was as she approached that the magic began to work. The words he was about to speak ('Madam, you should not permit your son to play with his ball in this place') somehow got lost and quite other words came from his lips. 'Do not distress yourself, Madam. No harm done. That's a fine

child you have,' as with a smile he walked on. The proper apologies made and politely received, they parted, she rather surprised at such an amicable reception from The Recluse and he still with the traces of a smile on his lips.

'We might have had a child like that one' he thought, 'she would have been a wonderful mother.'

As he neared his own rooms he passed those of a colleague who was standing at his open door. Normally there would have been no recognition and none was expected. But this time the magic took hold again. 'Evening, Scott, enjoying the lovely air?' Dr Scott quickly replied to the unwonted greeting, 'Yes, wonderful evening, isn't it. Beginning to get a bit chilly now though.' Then he added, surprising himself as the magic took hold, 'Why don't you come in for a glass of port – I've got some good stuff.' 'Thank you, I'd like to.'

The two men went up the stairs together into the typical academic's room, books and papers everywhere and rather stuffy.

Dr Scott apologised 'Sorry it's a bit stuffy, my things get blown all over the place if I leave the window open.' With a sweep of his arm he swept the contents of a chair onto the floor. 'Sit you down and be comfortable while I get the glasses.'

Their talk flowed amicably, at first on everyday and commonplace topics – the weather, college management, Government and (of course) today's undergraduates. 'They are ignorant outside the set syllabus.' 'They don't think they need to know much else.' 'I spend half the first term telling them things they ought to have learnt at school.' 'But they rush off from meals to the television.'

'They never dine in Hall where they might hear some useful discussion except when they absolutely have to.'

But soon the two men were on to the subjects which interested them more – classical archaeology, recent finds in the Dead Sea and Greek philosophers.

The clock struck twelve and the professor jumped to his feet. 'Good gracious! I'd no idea it was so late and I've a nine o'clock lecture tomorrow. I want to add a few thoughts, mostly taken from your remarks, Scott, and I hope you don't mind. Well, it's been a very pleasant evening. Thanks a lot.' 'I'll come down the stairs with you.'

The two men stood at the open door for a few moments enjoying the balmy evening air. 'I found our discussion most stimulating,' Dr Scott said. 'You must come again.'

The magical day shot its last bolt as a cloud drifted over the glittering moon and The Recluse, who had issued no social invitation for decades, said 'No no no, my dear man. You must come to me next time. Let me be your host.'

An Extravagant Christmas

It was a pleasant sunny December morning, though cold, and the Lady Elaine was taking some fresh air on the terrace of her parents' ducal castle. They had exchanged greetings and presents. Awaiting her marriage, the lady was a bit pensive. She had heard nothing from her true love, and could not communicate with him as she did not know where he was – only that he was on some confidential work for the king. She thought ruefully, he might at least have sent me some token.

Presently, a cart drew up on the terrace with two men, aided by the gardener who had broken into his holiday to see to his cherished house plants. They unloaded a heavy tub full of mould, with a small bare winter pear tree. On the top branches was balanced a beautifully-executed model of a partridge, carved from light wood and coloured correctly.

On the second day of Christmas the same operation was repeated, with the addition of a pair of turtle doves in a cage. The Duke said: 'You know those disused dovecotes in the park? Have the birds taken there.' The birds were housed in one of the dovecotes and thus was the second day done.

Elaine was beginning to wonder what the third day might bring forth. It turned out to be an exact repetition of the second, with the addition of three calling birds. The Duke said he would have only one of them in the castle aviary, they were so noisy. The other two must go to the local zoo.

The fourth day, in addition to the pear tree and birds, brought four French hens which went to the castle farmer.

On the fifth day there were five gold rings. These, in their pretty basket, were quite an acceptable present. Elaine slipped one on her own slender finger and let the rest stay where they were, to be joined by any more which might arrive on the following days. She went to bed that night in a peaceable state of mind, but very much wondering what the next day might bring forth.

The sixth day's gifts were not well received – six closed baskets occupied by six geese a-laying, followed by the now-familiar train of gifts. The Duke again despatched the geese to the farmer, who shut them into a distant outhouse. The farmer was much annoyed at having to open up his closed outhouse for their accommodation.

On the seventh day of Christmas, everyone was pleased to see seven swans swimming on the castle moat.

On the eighth day, as well as the usual paraphernalia, eight drummers arrived – drumming. Everyone within earshot stopped their ears, and the drummers were immediately marched off to the barracks. The Lady Elaine was awake most of the night wondering what further awful presents the ninth day might bring forth. .

On the ninth day, as well as all the other gifts, nine pipers were seen perspiring up the drive. The Duke decided that it would be pleasant to have one man only playing Scottish airs on the terrace where they were having their meals. Some people do not care for bagpipe music. The other pipers followed the drummers to the barracks.

The next day was not unpleasant. There appeared, followed by the train of previous gifts, ten maids a-milking with their attendant cows (or in some cases goats). The farmer was quite pleased by their arrival, for he was relying on their production to make up the milk deficit which he had foreseen while the castle was full of guests. Also, he was short of staff and some of the maids agreed to stay on instead of going home.

Elaine was feeling distinctly restless and quite unable to guess what the eleventh day could possibly bring forth. On the morning of the eleventh day, eleven young ladies came to coffee. 'Now, surely, tomorrow will be the end,' thought Elaine, 'it is the twelfth day of Christmas. But I do wish I could get in touch with my love himself!'

On the morning of the twelfth day Elaine smiled, for evidently the Prince had failed to persuade twelve young and active lords to leap up the avenue and his twelve lords a-leaping included some gray heads who could hardly lift their feet from the ground. They were all led into the castle, followed by eleven more grand ladies and all the usual train of gifts. Last of all came the Prince himself, her true love, on a gaily caparisoned and lively horse. Up he came to her, expecting an absolutely rapturous greeting and thanks, and he was slightly daunted by her cool reception. She was not impolite, but far from rapturous.

The Prince and his Lady Elaine were married with great pomp in the castle chapel by the archbishop, attended by twenty-two young ladies and twelve lords. To each of them, Elaine had previously given one of her forty gold rings, as well as giving one to her mother, while the gentlemen also received various turtle doves, calling birds or swans – even in one case a goose – where they could provide suitable accommodation.

I would like to be able to conclude this account in proper fairy tale style by saying they lived happily ever after. Alas, it is not possible. For the most part they were content enough, living in their wing of the castle. They reared a family of healthy children there. But if ever any mishap occurred in the castle, park or farm, which could be set down in any way to his foolishness at that Christmas, Elaine would never fail to remind her husband in pointed language how silly he had been. One of those occasions was when a goose got out of its enclosure and hissed at the farmer's little daughter and caused a nasty fall. The Prince never became a favourite son-in-law of the Duke and Duchess, who could not forget his silly presents on that extravagant Christmas.

The Elf

It was a bright summer morning some two or three hundred years ago, and the sun had recently risen on a quiet village street that was just waking up. A cat lay sunning itself on a door step, keeping a wary eye on a dog nosing for scraps at the door of the just-opened butcher's shop. A small being might be seen, sitting on a chimney pot and looking around with interest. Smoke began to rise from some of the chimneys and soon the small being might be seen fidgeting. His seat was becoming smoky and uncomfortable. The small being wriggled uncomfortably as his seat became warmer and then said to himself 'It is time I moved on.' He slid over the roof, dislodging tiles in his progress, then down a drain pipe, and walked the short distance to the garden gate.

A girl approached him from the opposite direction. 'Hello,' she said, 'who are you? Who do you belong to? I don't think I've seen you before.' 'I don't belong to anybody but myself. I'm Simkin.' 'Who looks after you, then?' asked Nellie. 'I look after myself, of course!' 'But you're too young!' 'No, I'm eleven,' replied Simkin. 'You can't be – you look about four!' Simkin laughed. 'Well, I am. You know, I'm an elf, and we are smaller than you humans. How old are you? What's your name?' 'I'm Nellie. I'm twelve years old. Are you really an elf?'

Just then, a man came out of the newly-opened butcher's shop carrying a covered tray with a delicious smell. Taking a penny out of her purse, Nellie ran towards him saying 'A pie, please!' Simkin followed, also holding out his hand and saying 'A pie, please!' Simkin looked puzzled when the man replied 'Come along, laddie, where's your penny?' 'What's he mean, Nellie?' 'Your money!' The elf could produce no penny, but Nellie found another coin and said: 'I'll buy you one.'

'Now please,' said Simkin, when they were seated on the bench enjoying pies, 'about the pennies – what are they?' 'Money of course,' she replied. 'But what is money? I don't understand!' 'I'll explain,' Nellie said. 'You get money for wages, or from the bank' She explained about wages, but when she tried to explain about banking she found it too difficult and was completely defeated. 'Yes, I think I see,' said Simkin, 'but how do you get this money?' 'What do you do, then?' she asked. 'Ours is a much better system. We still go to school for reading and writing and arithmetic and Elf History. Then if we want to we move on to training school when we are grown up. I hope then to become a farmer. Oh dear, what shall I do here without any money?' 'Go back, I suppose,' said Nellie. 'I can't! You see, I was so anxious to see Earth that I came down when I had done the first part of the course but not the bit about getting back!'

'That is a problem,' Nellie said sympathetically, and really miserable. Simkin looked thoughtful. 'Oh, I know! Didn't you say you wanted to be a farmer? Well, my Father is a farmer and has just had to dismiss his bird-scaring lad because he was lazy and incompetent. He's looking for another. Perhaps he'd employ you. Would you like that?' Simkin brightened. 'Oh, it would be interesting to study farming methods. I want to be a farmer,' he replied. 'Come on then' she said, and they went up the village.

Not far away they found Mr Wilkes on his cornfield which had been wrecked by the laziness of the last lad. He was not in the best of tempers. He was interested to meet Simkin, but thought he would not be strong enough for the job. Simkin soon demonstrated that he was very strong, by turning over a cast sheep which had fallen on its back and was unable to get up. In the end, Mr Wilkes gave in to the pleading of the two of them. Simkin was engaged for a penny a day (worth a lot more then than now) and could sleep in the barn where there were plenty of sacks and rugs. He would have to be on the job early, and someone would bring him out some breakfast, while for half an hour for lunch he could come into the farm house for a proper meal.

Suddenly, with a flash and a bang, someone materialised. 'Oh, that's my teacher, Grimalkin,' cried Simkin. He rose and bowed low – 'Welcome, Sir.' Nellie also rose and gave greeting in the manner of one welcoming a guest. Grimalkin was fond of children, but he turned a stern look on Simkin. 'Now then, what are you doing here, you very naughty boy?' 'I was looking, Sir,' said Simkin, with a penitent expression. 'Don't prevaricate! You know very well what I mean.' 'Sir,' Simkin replied, 'I so longed to be on earth!' 'That's no excuse. You are coming back with me now!' Here Nellie broke in – 'O Sir,' she cried, 'he has got work on the farm for Father, who would be so sorry to lose him!'

After desperate pleading from the two of them, and explanations of how difficult it would be for Mr Wilkes to find a replacement, Grimalkin kindly agreed to grant a week's grace. He would come again at the same time, and then Simkin must go! This caused much consternation, and Mr Wilkes was quite angry: 'It all comes of employing foreigners!' he said. A further extension was granted on the next visit.

Every year, during Nellie's school holidays, Simkin would stay a week on the farm as a guest. This continued for some years, and then both developed other interests. Simkin became much interested in Elfland farming methods. Nellie, as she grew older, acquired human boy friends. But although she rarely thought of Simkin, she never quite forgot that once she had been 'best friends' with Simkin, the Elf.

A Family Christmas, or 'Here We Go Round the Mulberry Bush'

Christmas bells rang out joyously from the tower of the old village church as the congregation streamed out into the frosty air followed by the vicar with whom they exchanged greetings, greeting friends and acquaintances and then turning away to make their way home and enjoy their Christmas fare. The Wilkeses were there with their three children and Mrs Wilkes's widowed sister Mrs Sarson with her two children. They all started on the walk home.

Just as the Wilkes party started homeward, Matthew Sarson went up to Mr Wilkes saying in a plaintive tone: 'Uncle Peter, where's the car?' 'At home, of course, where we left it.' 'But I'm freezing.' 'Don't be so silly, Matthew, the walk will warm you up…' 'But I'm freezing.' 'Run about then and get warm.' By now Matthew's sister Kate had joined in as well as the younger Wilkes children. 'I'm freezing too, Uncle Peter!' Mrs Sarson called to them: 'Children! I'm ashamed of you. Behave yourselves. I don't know what's got into you.'

It certainly was a most lovely day. The air was crisp and frosty and the wintry sun glimmered and shone on the frost-covered ground, with a slight dressing of snow. However, the murmurings went on all the way home and there was a rush for the door while Mr Wilkes was fumbling in his pocket for the key. Mrs Wilkes, standing near her husband as he opened the door, pronounced firmly: 'No grumbles in the house on Christmas morning. Run about to keep warm and when you're not grumbling you can come in.'

'I'm not grumbling, Mother' said John, the eldest boy. 'No, I know you're not. Come in now if you like.' 'Hang on a moment, John' cried Mrs Sarson, 'Will you stay out with me and help me with the grumblers?' 'Of course I will,' replied John, an active teenager always ready to take part in an active ploy and to help. 'What do you propose to do with them, Auntie Joyce?' 'Run them off their feet till they're boiling instead of freezing – come on!' She took them down to the mulberry tree on the lawn and formed them into a ring round it. 'I'll take Tim in my right hand and I can help him if we go too fast. You go opposite at 6 o'clock and take Rosie in your right and Kate in your left. Kate can hold Tim's hand and Rosie take Matthew's.

They made a ring round the mulberry bush and started going round, at first slowly. Mrs Sarson and John sang as the rest were sulking but Rosie soon followed her beloved big brother's lead and persuaded the others to do the same:

Here we go round the mulberry bush
The mulberry bush, the mulberry bush
On a cold and frosty morning

so they went round and round and round getting faster. Then the direction was reversed to anti-clockwise and they sang such carols as they could remember – faster, faster, till Rosie panting and gasping cried out 'Oh Auntie Joyce, do stop! I shall collapse soon.' Mrs Sarson gave the word and they rushed back to the house, laughing and panting 'I'm boiling, I'm boiling.' 'Come in,' cried Mrs Wilkes. She snatched up her little Tim and kissed him.

'Now for presents,' cried Matthew, only to be repressed by John: 'Don't be a stupid ass, you know we have dinner first.' 'Sorry, I forgot that' said Matthew, but he did not sound very sorry. They all went into the dining room where Mr Wilkes was waiting while the finishing touches were completed in the kitchen. There were decorations of holly and flowers on the table, and a cracker by every place. A portion of smoked salmon was laid out for a starter. The crackers were fat and beautiful.

'No cracker-pulling till the pudding comes in,' said Mr Wilkes. 'Oh, Father' said Rosie, 'We know that!' 'You may,' replied her Father, 'but Tim may not. Do you remember last Christmas, Tim?' 'No!' the

little boy replied stolidly. 'Kate, what about you?' 'Not very well,' said she. 'Well then, I'll go on. Listen, Tim. When the pudding is coming in, burning, we all take our crackers in our hands to join with our neighbour on the other side to make a circle and all pull at once. Now, eat your starter slowly. The ladies want a bit more time in the kitchen.'

They all began. Soon the children, with the exception of Tim, had finished their starters and were growing restless. Tim was not sure if he liked smoked salmon and was only nibbling at it. Mr Wilkes had not touched his and was wondering how he could amuse them.

'You remember that Latin Grace I sometimes use?' 'Yes' said several voices. 'Do you know what it means?' 'No.' 'Right, well…' and he went through the words. 'Now in translation, please! 'I don't quite understand the first bit, Dad.' 'Right' said Mr Wilkes. 'Matthew?' 'We don't do Latin at school, Uncle Peter.' 'More's the pity!' and he translated.

'Now,' he went on, 'what about the old Scottish one? It starts: "Some hae meat but canna eat." What do you understand by "some", Rosie?' 'Some people, Dad!' 'Right. Now, Katie, "but canna eat", Kate?' 'Now, "meat"?' 'Well, that's obvious Uncle Peter,' Matthew said confidently, 'we all know what meat is.' 'That's just where you're wrong…' 'I think,' said John rather doubtfully, 'it might mean food in general.' 'I think so too,' replied his Father. 'So now we have "Some have food but canna eat". "Canna"?' 'Can't,' said Kate. 'Good so far,' said Mr Wilkes, 'Now, please, "And some wad eat that want it"?' 'Well, everyone wants food,' said Matthew. 'I think there's more to it than that,' said John. 'What do you think it means, then?' asked his Father.

What's the last sentence?' 'Well,' John said, 'I suppose it means some people would like to have a meal but don't possess the necessary supplies.' 'I think that too,' said Mr Wilkes. 'Well, Kate, what about "we hae meat"?' 'I suppose,' Kate ventured, 'it means "we've got food"?' 'Right! Yes, and the actual word here. Right again! Next line, Matthew? "We've got food and we can eat so let the Lord be thankit"." 'Be thanked,' said Matthew, 'let the Lord be thanked.'

'So – now let's have the whole thing in a nice plain sentence that the ordinary English person, ignorant of Scottish dialect, would understand.' John began: 'Some people have food but are unable to eat it and some people would like to eat but are lacking supplies but we have food and can eat it so thank God.' 'Right,' said Mr Wilkes, 'although perhaps it might be more elegantly phrased. And I'm not quite sure I got the original words exactly right.'

The children were now getting restless for the next course of lunch as all the starters were gone with the exception of Tim's – who was still wondering if he liked smoked salmon – and Mr Wilkes'.

At last… Mr Wilkes carried in the turkey, which he could hardly lift. 'Gee, what a monster!' remarked Matthew, 'I shouldn't like to meet that gobbler on a dark night.' 'John,' said Mr Wilkes, 'next year I think I'll get you to help carving. I'll hardly get any myself by the time you lot are fed' 'Oh Dad, I'd love to,' cried John. 'Good, well watch me. Carving is an art – you don't just chop bits off but first take out some nice slices, along the breast.' John obeyed and Mr Wilkes set to work, telling a story of an old lady who said she'd never tasted breast of chicken because when she was young the first portions had always gone to the grown-ups and now she was old they were sent first to the children.

Large as it was, the bird was beautifully tender having been cooking all night in a slow oven and browned on high heat after they got back from church. The sprouts were just right, and the potatoes crisp, and there was a new addition that year in the shape of red cabbage. Everyone fell to and Mr Wilkes managed to get his share. Then willing hands cleared the plates and stacked them in the dishwasher.

Mrs Sarson lowered the lights while Mrs Wilkes brought in the pudding, its blue flame rising to heaven. Then she explained again to

Tim her method of serving Christmas Pudding, in spite of murmurs from the others of 'We know, Mother'. The pudding was made to an old family recipe, served with brandy butter. 'You see, Tim' said his Mother, 'I cut slices in regular order and serve straight round the table even if I see treasure peeping out of the next slice. There is no cheating. The treasure is charms from a card and some precious silver threepenny bits which come out year after year. I want to get them back for next year, and if one falls to your lot, Tim, I'll buy it back for £1 in today's money. Be quiet, Rosie, I know you know but I'm telling Tim!' To his enormous joy, Tim got the first threepenny bit; Mr Wilkes, to general applause and laughter, got a bachelor's button; Rosie a little donkey.

After the pudding had been enjoyed they turned to the pretty bowls of fruit, tangerines, crystallised fruit, Chinese figs, large raisins and chocolates. Then Mr Wilkes disappeared while the rest cleared the table and set it ready for the later supper.

Then, all migrated to the living room. Mr Wilkes was already there and had brought in two large waste paper baskets for torn wrappings. He was in the guise – one can hardly say disguise – of Father Christmas, in an old red dressing gown and a cotton wool beard which was soon discarded because it got into his mouth. Every one of the party of eight had given something to the other seven so, if my arithmetic is correct, there should have been fifty-six parcels on the floor round the tree. This total was slightly reduced by the 'big' presents being often given jointly by parents, aunts or uncles, and then added to by postal packets from absent grandparents. But there must have been about fifty still. The Wilkeses were not rich people and even the big presents were not – as in some families – a motor bicycle or even a car, but they were always something that the child wanted and had probably asked for. Thus, John got the larger cricket bat as he had outgrown his last season. He turned to his cousin Matthew and said: 'You can have my old one if you like, Mat, I can't wait for Tim to be old enough.' Kate got her longed-for dolls' pram from her mother and aunt jointly, with a beautifully cover embroidered by her mother, and Rosie, who had recently taken up art seriously and shown talent in that direction, received a beautiful new paint box, a sketch pad and a pile of very good paint brushes. For a while the air was noisy with 'Just what I wanted!', 'Thank you very much', and people running about to kiss a donor.

Mrs Wilkes was enjoying a well-earned after-lunch nap when Mrs Sarson jumped up, crying 'Who is for a short walk before it is quite dark? It will settle the wonderful lunch and make room in our tummies for Christmas cake.' John cried 'I'm your man, Auntie Joyce!' Rosie followed the adored older brother and Matthew rose reluctantly under the stern eye of his mother. Mr Wilkes joined the party and they set forth.

Mrs Wilkes opened sleepy eyes and, with her usual hatred of waste and sense of economy, began to rescue such large bits of wrappings as could be ironed over and used on another occasion. She then went to prepare the tea trolley. The walking party returned glowing and the trolley came in. Rosie, who had iced the cake, invited everyone to admire her handiwork. She knew her brother John's tastes, and quickly said to him 'I'll eat your marzipan, John.' Kate ran out of the room to fetch her doll and install it in the new pram. Then for a while there was comparative peace in the room. John was in a corner practising forward strokes against an imaginary bowler and Matthew, in another corner, waving rather dangerously the new tennis racket he had received from his uncle and aunt. His old racket had belonged to his dead father and was still too heavy for him.

The next traditional occupation was Carols, chosen in order of age starting from the youngest. Tim chose *Away in a Manger*, the only one he knew. When it came to the carol *As Joseph was a-Walking*, and the verse which says 'Light you up your candles this night of all the year', the real wax candles on the tree were lit, carefully watched by the grown-ups.

Carols were followed by supper – a whole boiled ham, salad and mince-pies. Once again, the ham was expertly carved in thin slices by Mr Wilkes, who prided himself on his skill.

Tim was by now practically asleep and his father carried him up to bed followed by Mrs Wilkes who, after the scantiest of washes, popped him into bed where he slept soundly. The others started filling their hot water bottles and gradually drifted off upstairs, all declaring that this had been the Nicest Ever Christmas.

The *Flying Fisher*

Giles Fisher was an active young man who worked in London. He was extremely keen on sailing and had, fortunately for him, received a legacy which enabled him to buy a small yacht. He was immensely proud of her, tho' she was not a fast sailer. He called her the *Flying Fisher*. Mrs Ford from the village was employed to keep an eye on the yacht and clean up.

One day he received a telephone call from her in very gloomy tones. His mind immediately flew to what harm could have happened to his beloved yacht. 'Mr Fisher, such bad news!… it have got onto the boat.' 'Well, Mrs Ford,' he said, 'What's up? If this weather holds, which looks likely, I'll be down on Saturday, and if you need more cash I can pay then.' The next remark shook him badly. 'Oh no, Mr Fisher, Sir, it's not that! Such bad news!' 'Bad news! What could have gone wrong? A storm? A fire? What is it, Mrs Ford?' His mind immediately flew to what harm could have happened to his beloved yacht. 'What's got onto the boat?' Giles asked anxiously. 'Oh, Mr Fisher, a mouse have got on to your boat. A mouse have crawled up the tie-up string of your beautiful boat.' (It will be clear that Mrs Ford had not been in the village long enough to acquire the proper nautical term.)

I am sorry to have to say that Giles laughed, and returned a cheery 'Oh dear!' But Mrs Ford was not cheered. 'I do try to keep the boat nice for you. Oh, Mr Fisher, I do try to keep that boat nice for you, Sir, and now a mouse have got into it!! Oh dear, oh dear.' Giles returned a careless 'Buy a trap, Mrs Ford – or do you need more money?' He left her money for polishing and cleaning materials, which she used lavishly. 'It's not that, Mr Fisher, Sir, but it's the thought of that there nasty critter in your nice boat!' 'Well, cheer up Mrs Ford, and buy a trap.' Giles was by this time tired of the mouse and repeated: 'I'll be down on Saturday, if the weather holds.' 'Oh dear, oh dear, Mr Fisher Sir, it do worry me so.' Feeling rather tired now of the complaints, Giles cut off the telephone and Mrs Ford's moans.

It was a fine summer and Giles, often accompanied by his fiancée Wendy Wilson, went for most weekends to his beloved yacht. He had

named her the *Flying Fisher* because he was so besotted with her, but he really knew quite well that she was not a flier but rather a slow boat. Wendy shared his affections.

Giles, it must be admitted, was getting thoroughly bored with Mrs Ford and her complaints about the mouse, which did not bother him as much as it did her. 'Never mind,' he said, 'get as many mouse traps as you like and I'll pay you when we come down – which will be on Saturday if this weather holds. Miss Wilson and I will manage then.' 'But Mr Fisher Sir' pursued Mrs Ford 'I takes a pride in my work I does and it's not right that Miss Wilson and you should find your beautiful boat all messed up by that nasty little critter. I'll come in Saturday as usual.'

The weather held. The wind was good, and Giles and Wendy went down cheerfully on Saturday to be greeted by Mrs Ford with a most dismal face. 'Well, Mr Fisher Sir and Miss Wilson, I takes a pride in my work I does, and love it, and I don't like to think of you cleaning up here. It isn't right, Sir and Miss.' She then again offered to come in on Saturday mornings and help. 'If you do, Mrs Ford,' said Giles, 'I'll throw you into the water!' 'I must, Mr Fisher, Sir, it's not a right job for you or Miss Wilson.' 'Mrs Ford,' laughed Wendy, 'We can do it as well as you can. But it might speed things up if we bought another dustpan and brush.' 'OK,' Giles agreed. He was thinking of all the extra hours Mrs Ford already put in. 'If you do it we'll throw you overboard.' Mrs Ford actually laughed. 'If you does that, Sir, you'll find yourself in prison!' 'But he meant it, Mrs Ford,' said Wendy, who could see that Giles was getting really angry. 'Buy another dustpan and brush, that will speed things up. And you mind your step, Mrs Ford!' Mrs Ford grumblingly departed.

The following Saturday was again a lovely day, but they were again greeted by the sight of Mrs Ford's lugubrious face and grumbling words. 'Go away, Mrs Ford,' Giles said firmly. 'We'll do what's necessary today. 'And if we don't,' Wendy put in, 'We'll send that mouse for such a shaking up that he'll be glad to leave his quarters.' Mrs Ford at last went, and the two – laughing – did a superficial tidy up and sailed off.

The same proceedings were gone through several times during that lovely summer, and Mousie got quite accustomed to being rocked to sleep in his cosy concealed quarters.

One weekend was different. Giles and Wendy both had a week's holiday from work at the same time, and they decided to go for a longer trip than usual. When Mousie crawled ashore on the mooring rope as usual he found himself in strange surroundings. He did not know which way to go for his provisions, nor where were the runs of the local cats and dogs. And the people around him were talking a strange language. He looked about uncertainly and, luckily for him, met a little lady mouse called Mousiekin who had lived in England for a while and spoke some English. She showed him where to go, but Oh! What was this? – when they went back to the quay the *Flying Fisher* was gone! Giles and Wendy had taken advantage of the weather and gone further down the coast. The two mice conferred and Mousie stayed in Mousikin's hole till the yacht returned. Mousie then persuaded her to come with him for another visit to England.

Giles and Wendy met with a particularly mournful greeting from Mrs Ford when she found that the mouse population had doubled.

The lovely summer drifted on and there were many weekends on which Giles and Wendy got down for a sail and the programme with Mrs Ford was repeated. For although she bought many traps and baited them carefully and caught many of the young families, she never succeeded with the parents. And, until cold winter weather forced them to seek warmer quarters on land, Mousie and Mousiekin remained inhabitants of the *Flying Fisher.*

A Lonely Christmas

Vivienne stood by her window watching the cars while swirling snow was falling fast from a grey sky. She was pondering. The plan for this Christmas morning had been to walk the scant half mile to church and then, after a convivial drink of coffee with friends and neighbours, to go home with William Wilkes for a merry Christmas lunch with his wife Wendy and their family. She was an elderly lady, none too steady on her legs, and knew that the walk in this snow would be most unwise. Yet William, who was the church organist, would not be free to come and fetch her. When she had telephoned William he had explained that No, he certainly could not come, and his wife Wendy was nervous about driving in the snow with the children. The lane was narrow, and always the last road to be gritted. They could not attempt it while it was still snowing – with profuse apologies, of course, and promises to collect her for a meal another day. Vivienne had forced herself to sound cheerful, then flopped into her chair and collapsed into tears. It was too late to make other arrangements. Having no family, she was used to being on her own – but on Christmas Day!

She began to think of past Christmases. Her memory was not good, and the earliest Christmas Days were quite undateable, but she got a vague picture of lying in bed in the dark, rustling the crinkly parcels on her feet. They would have been brown paper parcels – no fancy paper in those days. Children did not have bedside lamps either, and to get to the overhead light switch at the door would have meant tumbling out of her warm bed into the cold and dark. Besides, crossing the floor meant that Nannie might hear and come up and be cross with her. So she lay in bed, kicking and fretting. After what seemed an age, Nannie did come in: 'Happy Christmas' she said, but then 'What are you doing awake at this hour?' 'I want some light to see by' Vivienne said, 'to see these parcels.' 'No indeed – not until your Father and Mother have been in. They'll be along quite soon.'

The memory faded. The next must have been a year or two later. That Christmas was remembered because of one present which she had particularly liked. That was a toy shop, made of stiff cardboard, and containing lots of little jars of foods which could be replaced from the kitchen when they were empty. They were filled with little goodies – small chocolates, tiny biscuits and raisins and sultanas. There were also some duller ones – sugar, salt and rice. Vivienne played with this for hours and her dolls had many a feast.

Then she remembered a Christmas spent in hospital once when she had been ill. The Ward was decorated, and sisters and doctors and those patients who were able all joined in singing carols.

She passed several Christmases at her boarding school while her parents were in India where her Father had gone to work. There were some other children in the same position but it was not particularly interesting and there were no parties.

Then there was one Christmas spent with Grannie and Granddad. Grannie was a great reader aloud and could do Scottish tales in the right accent. That Christmas was nice, but not very exciting.

Then there was one really glorious Christmas in India. Children were not great travellers in her young days, and often did not see their parents for years. That Christmas was lovely. Vivienne was petted and made much of by the servants and the chaplain's wife and there were other English children to play with and presents galore.

Then, a little later on, there was a very dreary Christmas back in England staying with a strict aunt averse to any merriment. Best behaviour all the time and no parties!

When Vivienne grew up she had gone to work in London. She had a mass of family, friends and acquaintances who had always asked her to stay with them and sometimes she had gone again to visit the strict aunt, who seemed more companionable now that Vivienne was older

and the age gap had narrowed. But her visits were not particularly interesting. Sometimes she stayed with her grandparents.

The aunt died and left Vivienne a lot of money with which she bought the cottage up the lane. She lent it to her grandparents who became established there, and filled it with their good furniture, and made friends in the neighbourhood. Later, even when the grandparents died and her Father retired from India, she was never alone for a Christmas meal. All the furniture had been left to her and the cottage became a charming home.

Vivienne had managed to call up her composure when answering William Wilkes cheerfully, but burst into tears as he rang off. At last she stopped crying, and roused herself sufficiently to switch on the radio. She found that a Choral Service (later than their own) was going on and she heard once again the message of the babe in the manger, filling her heart with the peace, hope, love and joy of Christmas. I will not continue to gloom, she told herself. I will go and get myself some lunch at one o' clock and dry my tears. I am determined that the rest of the day shall be a Happy Christmas, although I must admit that for me this has to be a lonely Christmas.

A Midsummer Dream

It was a very hot summer and Midsummer Day was hottest of all. Even the coming of darkness brought no relief. Charlie tossed and turned on his bed, unable to sleep. The bedclothes and pillows and his pyjamas were all on the floor and his water was all drunk. He could hear his parents' voices in the garden and called to his mother but she did not hear him.

She was coming upstairs at last and did hear his voice and came in. 'Why darling, what a mess you're in. What are you doing?' 'I can't go to sleep' (this was almost a wail) 'and I've drunk all my water.' She went to get him more, and when she returned he gulped it down. 'Attend to me, Charlie, I am going to tidy you up and you are to lie quite still. It is easier to go to sleep lying flat than thrashing about. Then, all you need have on the bed is one sheet and I will arrange it on your feet as I showed you, folded in three, so when it gets cold later on you can put your hand down and pull it up over you. Now, goodnight darling.' She kissed him and left him.

While his mother and Charlie were talking, a mischievous dream came down from dreamland and into the little boy's mind. 'Hello,' it said. He could hear it quite clearly and later found it could hear him too, but he never saw it. It went on: 'Are you too hot?' 'Much too hot,' said Charlie rather crossly. 'Would you like to go somewhere cool?' 'Of course,' Charlie replied, 'but I can't.' 'I can take you,' said the dream, 'Where would you like to go?' 'Iceland.' 'Dreamland is cooler than Iceland – but get on your bed and shut your eyes while we're moving.' Charlie felt his bed moving, and when he opened his eyes he was surrounded by a white expanse of snow and ice. At first the coolness was delightful but it soon became chilly and he was glad he had a suit of pyjamas on and glad also to pull up the sheet as his mother had arranged it.

Then his eye caught something moving and looking closely he saw that it was a large ferocious looking polar bear. 'O dream,' he screamed, 'take me away! It's a bear and I'm cold!'

'Well it worked,' said the dream. 'Now I will take you to another place, you'll warm up there and won't meet bears.' After some gentle movement, when Charlie looked again he saw sand hills. This was a

nice place, he thought, except for a wish for a little less scorching sunshine. Suddenly he noticed a pride of lions prowling nearby and screamed for the dream to take him away.

Charlie next opened his eyes to the pleasant rippling sound of running water under a thick canopy of green leaves. He liked the place at first, but then there was a splash in the river and a fierce-looking crocodile emerged and came towards him.

Then the dream said: 'I think Scotland next, we were there this summer.' Charlie opened his eyes to an enchanting moorland landscape. 'No crocodiles, thank goodness, or other dangerous beasts' – though the wind was so strong as to offer a slight chill after he had become so accustomed to the sun. 'I wish the wind would drop,' he thought, but when it suddenly did it brought a new horror.

As Charlie wriggled and squirmed in the cloud of midges which emerged he remembered his Aunt Mabel's remark, 'Nobody can imagine how torturing Scottish midges can be until they have experienced them.'

'What shall I do with you, Charlie?' said the dream, 'you're a perfect nuisance,' and then, after consideration, 'We'll try a ship next.' The bed was soon on the deck of a small steamer where the crew went about their duties without appearing to notice him at all. He was settling down to enjoy himself when the wind got up again and the boat began to pitch and roll, and Charlie immediately started to feel seasick. This time the dream sounded almost cross with him. 'I'm tired of you, Charlie,' it said, 'I shall take you home!'

It was pleasant to be in his own little room again. The dream flew away and Charlie sank into a deep and dreamless sleep from which he was wakened by his mother and a cooler fresher day next morning.

Parallel Lives

The two babies in the stork's nest opened their eyes on the same day and looked around with interest. There was not much to be seen, just tops of bare winter trees waving in the breeze, and Father and Mother Stork sitting on the edge of the nest.

Father Stork spoke: 'Babies,' he said 'Listen to me. You have opened your eyes on the same day and you must become human babies in the district for which I am responsible. Mother Stork and I will take you down to the two homes which are expecting you. The two homes are very different, and it is given to me to see a little of future conditions in each of them. One of you will live in luxury as a nobleman, but will be isolated and will not experience love or friendship. The other will live in poverty, but will be surrounded by warmth and kisses and will eventually find true love. Neither of you will live long.'

In the Baron's cold castle there was great excitement and some anxiety. The Baron and his delicate wife had been married a number of years and had not got any children, and the Baron himself was keenly anxious for an heir to his ancient family – preferably a son, who would be received with loud ringing of the castle bell and great rejoicings, but even a daughter would be received gladly. But the heir was all-important, as there were unlikely to be more children.

In his great hall the Baron was pacing impatiently up and down, taking occasional sips of ale from the tankard on the trestle, and sending occasional messages up to his wife's bedroom, asking for news and for permission to go up. For what seemed a long time, neither was granted. At last, an under-nurse approached. She stood in the door and spoke: 'My Lord, you have a son.'

He rushed forward exultantly, crying 'I will go up and see him,' but she still stood in the doorway. 'Not so, My Lord. My Lady is not yet ready to receive you.' He stopped perforce, stamped his foot, and muttered under his breath, but the woman heard him. 'You must bide a little longer, Sir' she said. He had perforce to yield and went back to his restless pacing.

It seemed to the impatient man like a long hour but was only about ten minutes before the longed-for summons came. The Head Nurse appeared and told him he might now go up. Dashing past her, he mounted the great staircase two steps at a time, followed by the panting woman, and rushed into the Baroness's elegant bedroom. There, he ignored his wife's outstretched arms and with a curt nod in her direction turned straight to the beautifully trimmed cradle nearby, where the sleeping babe lay. The nurse, gasping, followed.

He said to the Nurse: 'All is well?' 'Certainly, My Lord' she panted out, 'But see how My Lady wishes to present her son.' 'Bother My Lady,' the Baron muttered – under his breath as he thought, but the Nurse heard him. He turned then towards his expectant wife. 'Who said that, My Lord? I am glad and proud that at last I have born us a son.' 'It is good,' he replied, and taking from under his cloak a large jewel case he added: 'As is customary on these happy occasions, Madam, I bring you an offering I hope worthy of the event. In this case it is the family jewels for the mother of the family's heir.'

The case was so heavy that the Baroness immediately let it drop onto the pillow beside her. As the Baron opened the casket himself the wonderful jewels caught the light from the surrounding torches and there were gasps of admiration from all around. 'Husband,' the Baroness cried 'I can never wear such jewels as these. They are too great for me!' 'Madam,' his brow darkened. 'You shall wear them when you rise from your bed and come down to grace our board once more. Nothing is too great for the mother of my son.' 'Very well' she answered meekly, 'and I would like to ask you, My Lord, about naming our son.' His brow darkened again as he replied angrily 'You should know that eldest sons of my family are always Hugo.' 'I have long known it, Sir – but I asked myself whether in this case we could add a second name and call him Hugo Charles in memory of my dear dead brother.' 'What are you thinking of? He is Hugo!' Tears filled her eyes as she sank back onto the pillow.

The baby began to cry and the Baron turned towards the cradle. 'Nurse, Nurse' he cried 'Why do you not do something for him? What is wrong?' 'There is nothing wrong, My Lord' answered the Nurse. 'He is just exercising his lungs.' The Baroness pulled herself upwards, stretching out her arms. 'Give my son to me' she cried. The Nurse was in the act of picking up Hugo when the Baron turned fiercely on her. 'No!' he shouted. 'She shall not hold him! She dropped my jewels. She might drop my son. You may hold him towards her and she may bend her head. Then you shall take him to the nursery, and there he shall live, visiting My Lady for five minutes only every morning. This is my command. Is it understood?' Both women nervously assented, the Nurse looking with pity at the poor mother who was crying. She looked with sympathy at her. Even the foster nurse, a wretched village woman who had been torn from her own week-old infant to serve her master's child, felt sorrow in her heart.

The Nurses moved Hugo in his cradle into the adjacent day nursery. The Baron went himself downstairs to order the ringing of the castle bell which effectively prevented his worn-out wife from taking her much-needed sleep. He gave out celebratory drinks to all his retainers, and sent messengers to such of his relations as were within riding distance.

Hugo was installed under the governance of the Baron's sister, a woman of as hard and a heart and character as the Baron himself, the Baroness having been deemed too feeble for the task. His nursery was furnished with every luxury known at the time, and with warm wall hangings, decorated with pictures to please a child's heart.

In the luxurious nursery young Hugo was brought up. Indulged and encouraged by his Aunt, he bullied his attendants, kicked his little dog, and was insolent to his Mother on his morning visits. The only person he feared was his Father who, when at home, insisted that Hugo become a bold rider of his lively pony and a skilful archer.

At fifteen, Hugo, as the Stork had prophesied, was sent to the army officers' school for sons of nobility and gentry. He had met few children during his youth, but every now and then his guardians had decided to invite children to visit him. These visits were not enjoyed by the guests for Hugo always insisted on choosing what games they should play and usually managed to win them.

At the army school he soon became as unpopular as he had been with his youthful guests. The lads were of course taught to fence, but only with blunted swords. Duelling with sharp ones was strictly forbidden. Hugo was so offensive to a fellow cadet that the latter challenged him to a proper duel. They enlisted their fellows as seconds and stole sharp swords from the armoury. One morning early they crept out unobserved with bitter hatred in their hearts. After fighting for some minutes, Hugo – the youngest and least experienced – received a death wound. He was not much missed or regretted, his father's hard heart holding only pride, not love. But his gentle mother still cherished love for her son in spite of his bad behaviour and mourned him deeply – as also did his ill-used little dog.

So ended the unregretted life of Hugo before his eighteenth birthday.

And now for the story of the second baby in the storks' nest, the little girl. Although, as the stork had prophesied, she was born into poverty-stricken circumstance, she was to live in a happy family full of singing and sunshine, thoroughly unlike Hugo's.

Her home was in the family of Adam, the Baron's head forester. The Baron was a mean employer and a bad landlord and the cottage was in poor repair. Adam and his hardworking wife Eva had done what they could to repair its crumbling walls but the roof was beyond their slender resources. The winter wind and rain crept in and the only warm room was the kitchen. Wood was never in short supply, however, and there was always a glowing fire.

Here Eva's bed had been moved in preparation for the looked-for birth, with beside it the crude cradle carved many years before for their older children. There were a number of children, all eagerly looking forward to the arrival of a new little brother or sister. Eleanora – as her parents named her – was welcomed with joy and laughter and a shower of kisses.

Eva's bed was soon removed and she was up and about. It had been cluttering up the small kitchen. But the baby's cradle still lay on the floor, near the warm fire. The little one was strong and healthy like the rest of the family, and soon tumbled about the house and garden with the other children. Eleanora learned quickly to avoid the fire, after she had once tried to catch a pretty spark.

So she grew, and the happy years passed uneventfully for some time. She never went to the village, the mother preferring to do the necessary economical shopping.

Eleanora found that her preferred work was the garden and she was generally busy there, picking up knowledge from various sources and becoming quite expert.

Her eldest brother was already working with his father and the eldest daughter was apprenticed to the village dressmaker. Once, she had been given a few days holiday to help her mother. She had also been given some offcuts of brightly coloured material, over which she had toiled for many hours to fashion a little dress which would fit the small sister for two or three years after she became a toddler. The two working children sent home what money they could spare from their meagre earnings to help out the family funds. Boots could only be afforded for the parents and the workers themselves. All other money was spent with the utmost care by Eva on her weekly trips to the village for household necessities. There was none left for boots for younger children who all went barefoot in passed-down clothing.

The little Eleanora, the second baby from the stork's nest, had to do likewise when she grew out of the one pretty dress the elder sister had made her. When old enough, she was taken to church on alternate Sundays. She and her sister looked after the new baby and plaited sandals of sorts out of dried rushes and grasses. These would not stand up to the long walk, and meant a pause to fasten them together with rushes before entering the dark old church.

So the years passed – happy, busy and uneventful. But one day, when Eleanora had become a ravishingly pretty young woman of fifteen or sixteen, an event took place which was to change the course of her life. The sound of a hunt was heard in the forest. This was not unusual in itself but as the sounds died away she looked up and saw a stranger approaching the garden gate, leading a gaily-caparisoned limping horse.

She went to the gate and greeted him. He returned her greeting with a courteous bow. 'How can I help you, Sir,' she said. He asked her the way to the village which she said she hardly knew. She offered to call her mother. Eva recognized the King's son Albert, and she and Eleanora executed beautiful curtsies. 'Your Highness,' murmured Eva, who had been before her marriage a lady's maid to an aristocrat and learned some courtly ways and manners. The Prince asked for shelter for his horse, which was exhausted, and to borrow a horse to ride home. 'We have no horse, Sir, only a rough pony not fit for you to ride, and he is out with my husband and will be tired out.'

When Albert had seen his horse safely ensconced in the shed, and warmly covered up with sacks – which were all this poor house could provide in the way of a horse rug – the Prince entered the cottage for a short rest before starting on the long way home. He added a request for the company of the charming daughter, while Eva begged to be excused as she had to prepare the meal for the returning family.

When Adam returned he at once offered to go himself. 'Stay' said the prince, 'Have some food first, and take this ring as a token of the authority of my orders.' His next request was for a bowl of the delicious smelling soup the others were drinking. 'I get nothing so good at the palace,' he added.

When the Prince had left Eva said: 'This will give us something to talk about – we shall not see him again!' But on the very next day he returned, bearing gifts. He brought fruits from the castle garden, white bread (which the younger children had never seen) and corn. Eva warned that the corn should not be given to the pony, which was unused to such fodder and might become uncontrollable. She said that she would give it to the chickens.

The Prince asked Eva if he might pay court to her daughter. Eva replied that she must consult Eleanora herself and her husband Adam. Eleanora said nothing.

Thereafter, the Prince rode over whenever he could escape from his duties and became quite expert at helping with the garden. Meanwhile, his Mother the Queen, becoming quite worried about this peasant's daughter on whom her son had set his heart, was wondering if such a one could ever be fit to join the Royal Family. She determined to see for herself. Prince Albert startled Eva by saying that the Queen was coming over to see them on the following day, in a closed carriage with two postillions. He added: 'She will remain in her carriage and Eleanora can get in to talk.' 'Oh No!' both exclaimed, 'This place is not fit for Her Majesty!' 'She will stay in her carriage,' Prince Albert went on, 'and you, darling, can get in and talk to her there.' There could be no refusal and the next day the carriage arrived.

Eleanora ran out, in a clean if shabby gown with her rush sandals on her feet, and got in. At first she hardly dared to open her mouth, but the Queen was so kind that she was soon talking quite easily. The Queen, for her part, was pleased with the girl. She said; 'I understand that you and my son wish to marry. Well, you will have to come and stay at the palace for perhaps a year, and learn to dress in appropriate clothing.' Eleanora in her shabby dress was driven to the palace, where she was provided with suitable clothes, thin stockings and heeled shoes.

As she had shown in babyhood, when one clutch at a flying spark taught her to avoid the fire, Eleanora was a quick learner. It was much less than a year when she was deemed fit to join the Royal Family, and she and Prince Albert were married amid general rejoicings. They took up residence in a wing of the palace, Eleanora soon learned to ride, and they went often to visit her parents who were now living in more comfort as the Prince's influence had induced the Baron to pay better wages to his employees and to improve their houses.

For Eleanora and Albert, in due course a baby arrived. Sadly, the infant Prince was born to fade as the following year began. So also failed Eleanora's health, and shortly before her eighteenth birthday she had faded away, deeply mourned by her husband and family and by the nation, which grieved for and long remembered its Pretty Princess.

A Quirky Godmother, or Almost A Fairy Tale

In her small old-fashioned fourth-floor flat in a poor and rough part of the town Marilyn Mason sat one evening poring over the stiffly embossed wedding invitation. Her best friend Ruth was getting married. The card was from Ruth's family – a family very unlike Marilyn's own family who were badly off.

Marilyn had already refused Ruth's invitation to be a bridesmaid, although Ruth had pressed her, saying 'But, darling – I'm buying the dresses you know. I want them all cut and made by my own dressmaker and exactly alike.' But Ruth had not considered the necessary accessories. Marilyn would have had to get new shoes and a new handbag and there would be the question of a wedding present. Ruth could not be given a tea towel! So, Marilyn could not afford to go – and she could not ask her parents: they were so badly off. Her mother was unable to work and her father was not at all well, and his cherished wish was that his only son, Marilyn's twin brother Max, should follow his Father's footsteps to his Oxbridge College. Oh no, she could not possibly ask him for any money. No, she really could not go. Her dear old handbag was disgracefully old-fashioned, her only decent shoes pinched her feet, and she had no jewellery.

Her pearl necklace – but its renovation was long overdue. It had been a coming-of-age present from her dear Godmother and was, she believed, genuine but this had been some time ago. Now, the pearls needed re-stringing. What if they burst in church and scattered everywhere – she would sink to the floor with shame! No, she must refuse the beautifully embossed invitation from Ruth's parents.

All the same, Marilyn took down from the shelf on which it lay the elegant casket in which the pearls lived, so as to have another look at them.

Marilyn looked once more at her precious pearls. She thought: 'I really must answer the invitation today, but I really can't accept.' Her pearls did indeed need rethreading. Her best dress was of the cut of yesteryear.

With a hasty movement, Marilyn rose to return the casket to the high shelf on which it lived. It slipped from her fingers with a crash to the floor. Bending to pick it up she saw, with horror, that the base had broken away. She saw that there was a small extra storage compartment beneath the bottom of the casket. In it was a wrapped packet and a letter in her Godmother's handwriting which ran:

> 'Dear Godchild,
> You know I am a Scot and am gifted with 'The Sight.' This leads me to believe that you will accidentally open this casket when you have special need of money. Don't put this letter back inside, for you will never be able to open it again. It contains instructions for pressing the proper levers to open the lock.'

Marilyn hastily put the letter behind her thin cushion and in excitement opened the packet. The precious jewels within, released from their long imprisonment, gleamed and sparkled in the poor light of her flat. She took up the letter again. It continued:

> 'These jewels belonged to my own Godmother who was a lady at the Court of the last Tsar of Russia. At the beginning of the Revolution she managed to get out, concealing one piece of her jewellery about her person. She thought that she could sell the jewels in England to support herself, but she found that she could not bear to give them up. Instead, she took a job as a mother's help, only occasionally getting out her treasure to look at it in private. My Godmother left the treasure to me, and I felt

the same – I could not bear to dispose of it. Now I pass it on to you. But in your case I suggest that you do dispose of the jewels. I do not think that they would be suitable for you to wear in your station in life. Indeed, it might even be dangerous to wear them in the rough district in which you live – you might be robbed or mugged. So you had better sell them.'

At a step on the stair, Marilyn jumped up and drew the scanty curtain over the window – although she realised that it was not likely that anyone would be looking in to a fourth floor window. She then recognised the well-known step as that of her boyfriend Roger. He came in shivering from the cold and rubbing his hands. He said quickly: 'Hello, sweetheart, get your coat and scarf quickly. Let's go to the Odeon. They are showing that new film we both wanted to see and we shall be just in time if you hurry.' 'No!' said Marilyn firmly. Roger's face fell and he looked put out. 'What do you mean, "No"? Aren't you well?' 'Oh, I'm fine, but I've something to tell you. Come in. Lock the door behind you and sit down.'

The strange story was then disclosed. At the sight of the treasure, Roger immediately looked up. He was a junior assistant in a very smart jeweller's shop in the West End where he was learning to appreciate fine stones. It was the kind of shop with wire over both windows and only one item on display at one time. 'Whew!' Roger said, 'You've got something here! I think these are absolutely wonderful.' 'So I thought,' pursued Marilyn. 'If you will stay with me tonight then tomorrow morning we can go to the jeweller round the corner and get something for them.' Now it was Roger's turn to say 'No!' and Marilyn whose face fell. 'Why?' she demanded. 'And can't you stay the night? I shall be frightened on my own.' 'Of course I'll stay the night,' Roger responded, 'but that man round the corner – he's no jeweller, he's just a shop man. He would not have any idea of what these are worth. I shall telephone my boss, then we can take them there.' 'All right, but let's go early, can't we? I shan't have a peaceful moment while they are still here.' 'No,' said Roger, 'Mr Lewis never arrives in the shop until 10o'clock. Then he has to see the staff and open the mail. It's no good our being there before 11.00. And now, sweetheart, you get undressed and go to bed properly and sleep. You are over-excited and tired. I'll stay on the sofa and keep watch.'

Despite her protestations, Marilyn was soon in a deep slumber which lasted until nearly 8.00. Roger ate a solid breakfast, but Marilyn could only take a cup of coffee and was fidgety until he said: 'Now – we can go.' 'Shall I put the jewels into my locking suitcase?' asked Marilyn. 'No,' said Roger, 'we want to leave the room looking as normal as possible in case old Mr Briggs comes snooping round. The jewel case will go safely in my pocket.' At last they were off.

When they arrived at the West End shop Mr Lewis saw them at once. Having an eye for charming young ladies, he expressed mild interest in their story but no more until he actually saw the jewels. Then he looked more closely, with a professional eye. 'You've really got something there, I believe, but of course each stone will have to be examined separately. If you will come back at the same time next week I will give you my verdict.' Marilyn's face fell. 'What's the matter, Miss Mason?' Roger quickly explained: 'My fiancée had been hoping for a small advance for the expenses of a wedding she has been invited to. But it's this weekend.' 'No problem,' said Mr Lewis. He pulled out his cheque book and wrote a cheque for a sum which staggered them both. 'This is far too much,' they both cried, 'You will lose on the bargain if the stones are not good.' Mr Lewis laughed: 'Not I, I am far too experienced a salesman to lose in that way. If all else fails, I could easily sell them as costume jewellery. Now, sit down you two, and I would like to get Mr Cartwright to come in and have a look.' Marilyn looked doubtfully at Roger, who quickly explained: 'Mr Cartwright is our senior assistant and has been with the firm for thirty years.' Roger then became confidential with his employer: 'I'm going to buy her an engagement ring, Sir,' he said. 'I hope one of ours,' said Mr Lewis. 'No,' said Roger, 'I can't afford them.' 'Sit down, let me go and make up a tray with Mr Cartwright of some which you could afford.'

Mr Lewis left the room and tipped Mr Cartwright the wink. None of the rings on display were rubbish, but among them he also put in two very special ones at a much reduced price – he knew well what Roger's salary was. Mr Lewis returned with the tray of rings and Roger immediately saw that the settings of two of them were far the best. He looked suspiciously, but did not dare to question his superiors. He guided Marilyn's choice to one of the better rings. Mr Lewis then telephoned the bank manger, who would otherwise be reluctant to pay out such a large sum to a person unknown. 'Now, if you will take my advice, Roger, make Miss Mason rest for a short time before you go shopping. And there is one condition.' Both looked a bit dashed at this, but Mr Lewis laughed: 'You must bring me one of the pretty things you buy to show me.' They all laughed and Roger and Marilyn went off to the shops.

Roger made Marilyn eat a good lunch, after which she bought all the things she needed for the wedding together with a decent block of writing paper on which to answer the invitation. Roger encouraged her to buy a worthy present for her friend Ruth. Then they went home. Marilyn's first task was to write – with many apologies – her belated acceptance of the invitation to the wedding and reception.

A week later they returned to see Mr Lewis and received a further cheque. The total amounted to a small fortune for Marilyn. She went straight off to make more purchases – a nice dress for her Mother (as she knew her size), two shirts for her Father, and for Max a case of mixed sherries and some cash to help furnish his college rooms.

Back in her house they encountered Mr Briggs, the nosey landlord. 'Where's that pretty box that used to be on your shelf? And I see you have a new curtain.' So he had been snooping round the flat! 'The bottom of the box was broken,' said Roger, 'and I took it to be mended.' 'I could have done that for you,' said Mr Briggs. 'It's already gone, thank you,' said Roger, 'and as for the new curtain, it is an engagement present.'

Roger and Marilyn sat down together for a light supper, making plans to get married the next year. Said Roger: 'We shall move to our own house in a nicer place – and always be grateful to your Quirky Godmother!'

The Sad Christmas, or The Tree

The Hedges were in their living room on a cold and misty Christmas Eve, drinking their after-lunch coffee. Sybilla looked up from her paper. 'Peter', she said. 'Yes?' 'You know we've never had a Christmas tree?' 'Yes, I know, of course. They've always been so expensive.' 'Yes, well I know that the big flower shop in the High Street is selling them off at half price – rooted with soil so they won't be shedding needles all over the place, so I thought it would be nice if we had one. What do you say?' 'Very nice – if you can carry the compost or whatever round to the car.' 'I can't by myself.' 'I'm afraid you must, darling. I'm not feeling all that good. I'll go upstairs and have a lie down. 'Oh Peter, you must come. I hate driving in the crowded streets just now!'

They argued like this for some moments before he gave in and, getting coats and scarves, they set out rather silently. He helped carry the things round the corner to the car park where another argument ensued – he would not accompany her to buy lights or decorations – which this time Peter won, firmly remaining in the car while Sybilla went off rather crossly shouting 'Lazybones!' at him as she went. Having of course been longer than she meant, when she returned she found Peter wrapped in the car rug and shivering.

The drive home was again a silent one, but he did help to carry in the heavy things and set them up. Then he put the car away and sat down to a cup of tea.

Presently Sybilla said: 'Now for the fun! Let's get decorating!' 'Not me', Peter answered. 'I'm off for my belated lie down – and a warm up' he added. Sybilla prettified the tree rather crossly and prepared their supper. Then she called up, but as there was no reply she walked upstairs thinking with some irritation 'He does sleep soundly but I'll soon wake him.' What was her dismay to find him in a disarranged bed muttering incoherently and evidently in a high fever.

Dismayed, Sybilla ran to the telephone to get the doctor. Their own doctor was on Christmas leave, and thus she got the partner whom she hardly knew. 'Well, bring your husband up here if you're worried, Mrs Hedges', he said cheerfully. 'I think he's delirious – I couldn't possibly get him in the car.' 'I've got a surgery full of people here.' 'Could you send a nurse for the night? 'Impossible', was the reply, 'they're all on leave or out on duty. I'll look over when I can and you will manage very well.'

Sybilla went back, intending to watch by her delirious husband all night, but was soon in a sound sleep from which she did not wake till the first daylight of Christmas morning was creeping in. Sybilla had never previously seen death, but the increasingly marble chill of his hands and face, and the flat and silent chest, told their own tale. With a cry, she flung herself upon Peter's body and lay there for a long time before forcing herself to telephone the doctor.[1] He, after the proper words of condolence, added that the surgery was full but he would come as soon as he could.

The doctor called at last and, as he went away, murmured below his breath. 'We knew he had this condition, and that this would happen some time, but he begged us not to tell you, Mrs Hedges.' Rashly, he added in a low voice (but sadly she heard him) 'I did not think it would have been so soon.' 'Oh doctor, I killed him! Chivvying him out!' 'No, Mrs Hedges, I don't think so. Don't say that.' Sybilla was not consoled, weeping bitterly as she went down to let him out.

For a moment she opened the living room door and looked at the pretty tree and then with a violent kick sent all flying to the floor – tree lights and decorations all went. Sybilla shut the door on the mess, and went upstairs again to weep away the rest of that Christmas Day.

---

1 On Christmas morning? Pre-NHS days, one assumes.

The young widow spent Boxing Day morning lamenting his death and blaming herself for hastening it. She took no food or drink, but later roused herself to telephone her mother – who replied with all expressions of love and sorrow. 'Oh Mother, come! Come soon!' 'Of course I'll come, but I can't come soon. Auntie Hester and Aunt Clare will be here tomorrow.' 'Leave them to look after themselves and

come!' 'No, darling, I can't. You haven't seen Aunt Clara lately. She had a stroke, you know, and she's incapable of looking after herself, and Auntie Hester has a long way to drive and must leave early. I'll come to you as soon as ever I can, I promise, but I suspect that Aunt Clara's family, who will be fetching her, are sleeping in after last night's jollifications with the telephone off the hook.'

Sybilla uttered a little moan and went upstairs again to resume her solitary vigil. It was nearly 1 o'clock before the doorbell rang. 'Oh Mother, how glad I am to see you! Will you have a little lunch? I can't, I can't, you see I killed my husband!' 'What nonsense are you talking?' was her Mother's reassurance. Her Mother tried scolding, and the voice of authority had its effect. 'Pull yourself together at once and come and have lunch.' 'I don't want any lunch! I can't eat!' 'Oh yes you can. I want some anyway. I've been very busy, and driven a long way.'

In the end, the voice of authority prevailed. Sybilla did eat a little lunch in the kitchen with her mother. Afterwards – 'I'll go upstairs again now'. 'No, now we'll have coffee in the living room.' 'No!' cried Sybilla, 'No!' But her mother had already opened the living room door and seen the tree all over the floor. Sybilla hung her head as her mother said 'My dear child, what is all this mess?' and Sybilla had to confess what she had done. She obeyed her mother's bidding to help clear up, before she was allowed to go upstairs again and mourn.

That Christmas, and many Christmases to come, were sad ones for Sybilla Hedges. She spent them lamenting the husband of her youth and blaming herself for hastening his death by her obstinacy – even though the doctor had reassured her that it was exceedingly unlikely to be so.

A Silly Queen, or 'Pussy Cat, Pussy Cat, Where Have You Been?'

You remember the honey Queen in the parlour? Some years before her time there was another Queen, a silly woman, in that same parlour. She was not only silly but very sentimental, without being thoughtful of the feelings of others.

One day this Queen had retired for her after-lunch nap. Court duties permitting, she always insisted on being alone. Lady Jane, her Lady-in-Waiting, was forced to retire onto a hard chair in the passage, struggling to keep awake and not fall with a bump to the floor. Suddenly, she heard loud shrieks from the Queen's parlour. Lady Jane rushed into the room to see the Queen standing in the far corner holding up her skirts to her knees and displaying a pair of bandy legs clad in scarlet stockings. 'Oh Jane' shrieked the Queen, 'A mouse, a mouse, came from under the lintel and eat crumbs – Oh, get the pest officer at once! No! Don't leave me! Oh! Oh!'

Lady Jane was considering how to obey these contradictory orders, when luckily for her a servant passed in the corridor. The servant went for Higgins, the pest officer. Higgins soon arrived. He was no respecter of persons and seeing that Her Majesty was still calling and crying out he exchanged a wink with Lady Jane, behind the Queen's back which nearly dissolved that Lady in giggles. All he said was 'What can I do for Your Majesty?' 'Higgins!' cried the Queen, 'a mouse, a great mouse! Can you get rid of it?' 'Easily, Ma'am,' replied Higgins, 'if you will retire to another room.' 'I must not do that, Higgins' replied the Queen, 'I will see this affair through!' 'It may take a little time, Ma'am'

Higgins then went off to collect his daughter's cat, with permission from the owner. He placed it in a covered basket which he laid on the Queen's lap. He gave strict instructions to Her Majesty not to let the animal go until he had made his dispositions. He had also brought along a wooden block which he could knock into place in front of the mouse hole when the animal emerged. 'Oh, the poor creature,' said Her Majesty, observing the cat, 'How thin it is, we must give it cream.' 'No, Ma'am,' said Higgins, 'certainly you must not till it has done its job, or it will take no interest.' 'Do you bandy words with me, man?' said the Queen. Higgins then sent the servant for cream from the pantry, and signed to Lady Jane to put it on a high shelf. This was done.

Higgins then checked that there was no crack under the door and stationed himself near enough to the mouse hole to knock the block into place. He ventured to suggest to the Queen that she should invite the tired Lady Jane to sit down, for which piece of impudence he received a haughty look from Her Majesty and a 'Mind your own business, man' – probably condemning the drooping Lady Jane to even longer on her tired legs. Higgins was no whit abashed, and made no other remark. The ill-assorted trio settled down to what might prove a long wait, Higgins remarking easily, in a low voice, 'Did you know that mice like apple peel, too, for bait?'

After several minutes the mouse emerged. On a sign from Higgins, the cat was released. It looked about and the mouse turned to retreat. Finding its hole blocked, it started to weave about looking for a way of escape, and was soon half hypnotised by the cat. Higgins put down his hand and caught the creature, and after a sign to Lady Jane to put down the cream to reward the cat he left the room, shutting the door.

Higgins took the cat home. It was joyously greeted by its family.

'Miaow, Ma' said the first kitten, 'where have you been?' 'I've been to London,' said the cat. 'What for?' said the second kitten. 'To visit the Queen.' 'What did you do there?' asked the third kitten. 'I caught a little mouse.' 'Where?' asked the fourth kitten. 'Under her chair!' 'Miaow, Ma,' said all the kittens, 'Let us snuggle up close and lick the remains of cream off your chin, and you shall tell us every single tiny detail of your journey to London to visit the Queen.'

Stephanie and Isla

People might have thought, and no doubt some people did, that she was a lonely child. Stephanie lived with her parents on a wild part of the Scottish coast by a deserted croft. There was no school and very few neighbours. Her Father taught her maths and French, and her Mother taught her history and literature, and took her for long scientific walks, and for many years she did lessons with them. Her parents were both writers. She was well educated by them and spent her leisure hours happily wandering the beach and making patterns of pretty shells and coloured seaweed.

After some years they thought she should have some young society and sent her to a smart boarding school in Edinburgh. Stephanie hated it. The girls looked down on her as a wild highlander and she despised them. She spent every term longing for the holidays.

One day during her holidays she wandered along the shore farther than ever before, to a previously unknown outcrop of rock. To her surprise she saw behind the rock a girlish head with a mass of golden hair. 'Hello,' said Stephanie. 'Stop!' said a voice, 'Are you alone?' 'Yes, of course. Who are you, and why are you living here? Why do you say "Stop"? I am only saying "Hello" to you.' Stephanie meanwhile was approaching the figure on the rock: 'Are you alone?' asked the voice again, and the head turned to look at her. 'I'm alone. I always am.' 'I've seen you often, and believe you.' 'But why are you so fussed?' 'Well, I'll tell you. You see I'm a mermaid and nasty men might try to catch me and put me in a zoo.' As Stephanie gradually came nearer, the voice went on: 'Are you sure there are no nasty men with you? They might want to catch me and put me in a museum.' 'Why on earth should anyone want to do that?' 'Well, not a museum but a zoo,' said the voice, 'You see, I'm a mermaid.' And a pretty face appeared through the hair and stared at Stephanie.

'People don't do that,' replied Stephanie firmly. 'But – a mermaid – I've never seen a mermaid. And why should anyone put you in a zoo?' 'They did my great grandmother, and people came and stared at her, and she had only a horrid little bath of stagnant water and she pined and died.' 'Oh poor thing,' cried Stephanie, 'but how do you know?' 'The birds told me. Yes, we speak their language as well as yours.' 'You speak ours well.' 'Better since we learnt how to make radio receivers under water. But come on up. What's your name?' 'Stephanie – what's yours?' 'Isla.'

Stephanie climbed up onto the ledge and found that the pretty creature before her was indeed a mermaid and with her tail in the deep water on the other side of the rock.

The two chatted pleasantly and became quite friendly. Then Stephanie looked at her watch and exclaimed 'Gracious! I shall be terribly late for lunch.' She darted off and Isla shouted after her: 'Come again tomorrow – and come an hour earlier if you can and we shall have longer.' 'All right, I will,' Stephanie shouted back. Her mother was not very particular about punctuality and luckily accepted Stephanie's explanation.

For several days the programme was repeated. Then one day Isla said: 'Stephanie, my mother would like to meet you' 'Will she come up and join us?' asked Stephanie' 'She can't,' said Isla. 'It's only we maids who live in both air and water. When we become women we are like you, the other way round. The men can never come.' 'Oh dear' said Stephanie, 'And I should like so much to meet your mother.' Isla looked at her reflectively. 'There is a way,' she said. 'My grandmother knows how.' Stephanie looked at her in surprise. 'There is a special capsule,' Isla went on, 'which will let you be with us for two or three hours. Grannie knows how to make it but the special seaweed is almost extinct.' Stephanie looked rather alarmed. 'I don't think I dare,' she said. 'It's quite safe,' Isla replied. After some persuasion, Stephanie agreed. 'Then come tomorrow,' Isla went on, 'with a swimsuit under your dress and bring a towel.'

Stephanie obeyed. When she reached the rock a grey head popped up for a moment and said: 'Shut your eyes and put your head under water and eat this slowly. I shall just be able to meet you but I can't stay long. I have to go to my other daughter who is not well.' Stephanie sucked the proffered pill, which was a kind of sweetie and tasted

delicious, and obeyed instructions. She thanked the mermaid's grandmother, who then swam off and was lost to sight.

Stephanie and Isla then swam together to a further outcrop of rock across the bay where Isla and her family lived. It was a pleasant cave, lit by a cleft in the roof, and with some fresh water flowing out of the wall of the kitchen annex. Her parents and her brother Orkney were already there. They sat on stalagmites with the tops flattened off and the table came floating in, propelled by a neat maid (a mermaid). The lunch was surprisingly good. It started with soup of red seaweed, the excess salt washed out, followed by little fishes and a green seaweed salad, and finished with a delicious pinkish seaweed jelly.

After lunch Isla said 'We must go! We have to see the King. He wants to meet a mortal.' 'Oh,' cried Stephanie, 'I don't know how to talk to a King. Do I have to call him "Your Majesty"?' 'He's very nice,' said Isla, 'he's quite a friend of mine. Say "Your Majesty" the first time, then an occasional "Sir" is good enough.'

While they were talking, a messenger rushed in saying 'Captain Orkney, Sir! Shark! Will you come please!' Stephanie blenched and trembled. 'It's all right,' said Isla. 'If they can't kill it the little sea horses will prick it with their rock swords until it goes away.' In this way, the sea horses drove the shark off and some then came to escort the girls.

The King's cave was very neat and very beautiful. The walls glowed with coloured jelly fish. 'Don't touch them,' warned Isla, 'they sting.' 'I know, my Dad got bitten on the foot by one and it took him ages to recover.'

The King was very welcoming and kind to Stephanie, having never seen such a sight before. She tried to curtsey, which was difficult in the water, and spoke up bravely. Soon Isla said: 'Come along, we must go back to the shore or you will be stuck here,' and they swam off. Stephanie returned home.

For a week or more Stephanie saw no Isla on the rock. One day, she went to the rock and saw a strip of rare seaweed with writing on it. 'A letter,' she thought as she picked it up. 'Wow! I shall know what's happened.' The letter was neatly written, but the spelling was extraordinary. She deciphered it and realised the meaning, however. The letter ran as follows:

> 'Dere Stephanie, we have gone to Greece. It's a nice place but the girls are toffee nosed we think. They think they are the whole of mer-history, and ours is nothing. I miss you a lot. Call me up if you ever go to Greece, your loving friend, Isla.'

'Oh,' thought Stephanie, 'Greece is a country. She doesn't know. She thinks it's a village near here. Even if we were to go there I'd never find her.'

For some days Stephanie was depressed. Then her father said that they were being taken to Greece for the Easter holidays. They had a very interesting time, because Stephanie's family were so knowledgeable, and the visit was very instructive.

When the weather began to get hot the family did go to the coast once or twice and Stephanie stole away, while her father and mother dozed in the deck chairs, and gave the special whistle she and Isla had agreed. It was to no avail, and when they went home she began to feel that her whole mermaid friendship had been a dream. Presently it was forgotten, and before very long Stephanie had ceased altogether to remember her friendship with Isla and soon ceased altogether to believe in the existence of an underwater sea folk.

Poem

Sitting in the sun,
My life's work done,
I'm thinking of you.
When we were young and bright
We could dance away the night
And go to work next day.
But now my hair is grey
And you are far away,
Safely in Heaven I pray,
And I can nothing do
But doze in shade or sun
Thinking of you.

M. E. F. Ll. S.
30 April 2005